CADY HAMMER

Chasing The Past

A Chasing Fae Collection

ISBN: 9781736886359

Editing by Angela R. Watts
Cover art by Milan Krstevski

This book was professionally typeset on Reedsy.
Find out more at reedsy.com

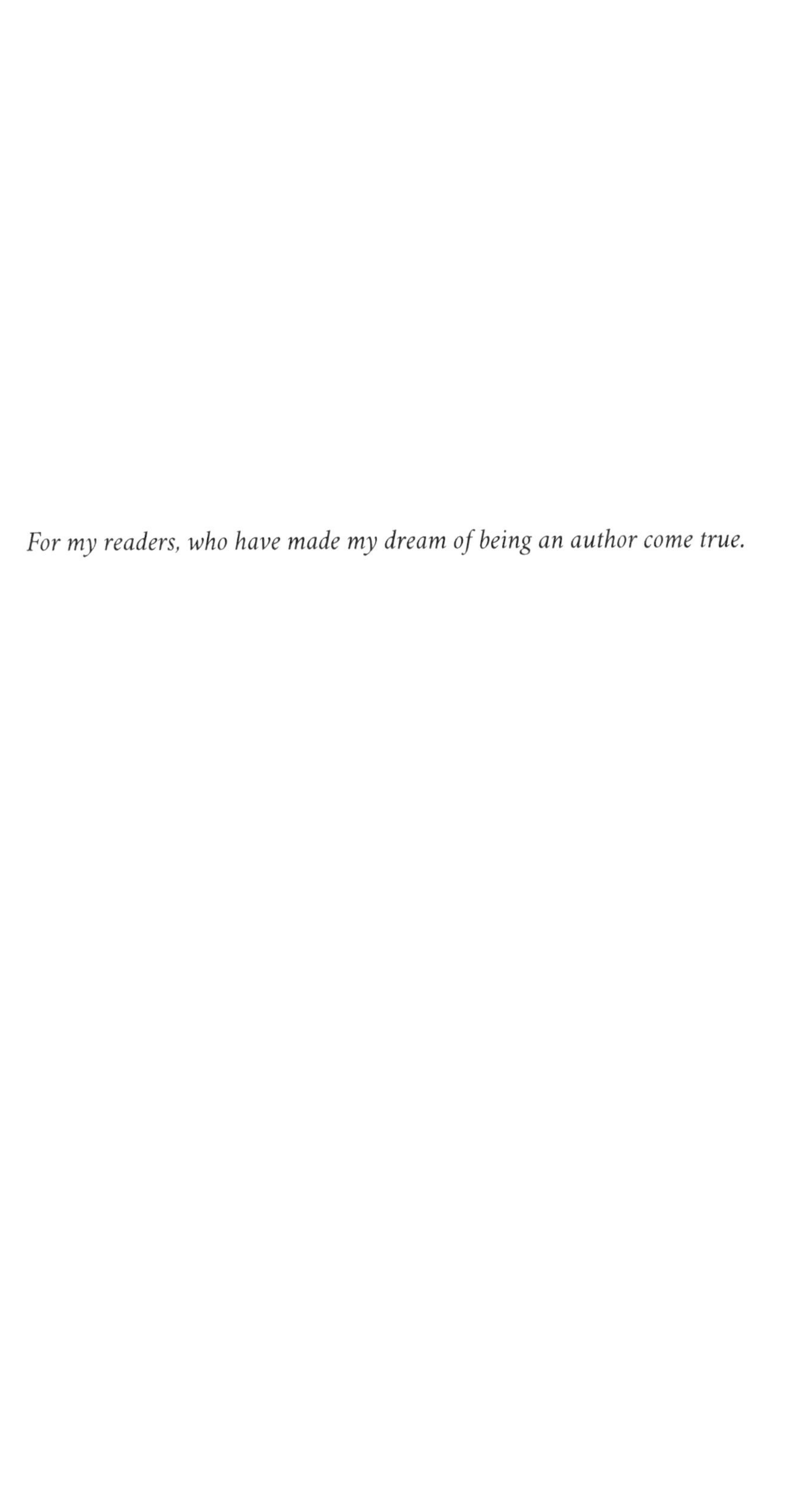

For my readers, who have made my dream of being an author come true.

I

A Chance Meeting

Alexander and Amelia's Story

I

Open paint night at Marlow Designs is my favorite night of the week.

Once a week, the art studio opens for artists of any skill level to come and paint for the night. The change of setting and support from fellow artists always inspires me to create my best work. The big open warehouse is the perfect place for a studio with its tall ceiling and exposed beams wound with string lights. It's simple, not too distracting, and brings your eyes to the huge windows that overlook Lisden in all its glory. You can practically get a panorama of the city. I bring my own canvases and set up shop here with all my paints and some of theirs. As always, I arrive right at the beginning, before the sun goes down, to maximize my time. Then I stay right until the last tinkling chime of the grandfather clock.

Tonight, I'm attempting to paint the city as the rain falls in heavy currents outside. It teams in buckets down on the buildings and creates constant streaks against the window glass. It creates this beautiful film and rippling effect over the image of Lisden's skyline. It makes the city look alive and in motion. As I watch the rain stream down, I draw my brush slowly over the canvas with a soft smile. *I just need to get this one spot...*

My thoughts are interrupted by the opening of the studio door. I turn around to see who has wandered in; I'm always excited to see another artist. To my surprise, however, an unfamiliar young man wanders in with his coat pulled high around his neck. His limp silvery hair hangs in his face as he drips water onto the tile floor. "Damn rain…" he mumbles gruffly. "Just came out of nowhere."

When he looks up, I can't help but let out a tiny chuckle. He looks a little silly, like a drowned rat.

"You must not be from around here," I blurt out. The man stiffens slightly as he looks over at me incredulously. His eyes scan the room before settling back on me. Trying to regain my composure, I quickly explain, "In Lisden, you always have to expect the unexpected storm." He shoots me a bit of a glare, and I feel awkward. *Maybe he's not a chuckling kind of person.*

I return a friendly smile. "I am… oh, I'm so sorry. I'm sorry for laughing. You look a little funny with your hair in your eyes." I motion my head towards the back room. "There's a few towels in the back if you'd like to dry off."

To my relief, the man sighs and turns up one corner of his lips lightly in a quarter-smile. "Could you bring them to me please?" He slides his hands into his hair and ruffles it, trying to shake some of the water out.

"Of course." *The least I could do really after my ill-placed quip.* I leave my paintbrush on the table before rushing to the back room to grab a few towels. I jog back over to him and hand them over. "Here you go." He runs one of the towels through his hair and rubs the other over his face. His whole demeanor brightens a bit as he adjusts to the much warmer temperature of the studio. "I'm Amelia. What's your name?"

"Alexander." He looks around the room again before staring at me a little more intently. "Where am I?"

I smile. "Welcome to Marlow Designs. It's open paint night. "But," I gesture to the mostly empty room, "it's been quiet today. Now, the rain must be keeping everyone away. Returning to my stool, I pick up the brush. "Do you paint?"

"No," he says as he moves over to me to set the damp towels on the end of the table. "I've never tried."

"Would you be interested in trying?" I pat the seat next to me. "I would be happy to share a canvas and some of my paints."

Alexander frowns slightly and shakes his head. "No, thank you. I'm not really interested in that kind of thing. I don't have a need for it. Paintings to me are… simply something to add to a blank wall."

I groan loudly. "Oh no… you're one of those." *I hate talking to art snobs.* "Paintings aren't just… objects to be hung on the wall and forgotten about. You're telling me you've never felt a connection with a painting or a feeling?"

"Never. They're expensive decorations to me; I've never seen them as anything else."

"*No*," I enunciate. "Oh, you can't think like that. Paintings are… pieces to be admired. To be enjoyed. To captivate the viewer." The man looks at me like he has no idea what I'm talking about. At least most of the other people I debate this issue with look like they couldn't care less, but this guy… he looks like he genuinely doesn't know what art represents. *How odd.* I feel this strange urge to teach him, to make him see.

With a wave of my hand, I motion Alexander over to the window. "Take a look outside. What do you see?"

He looks at me quietly for a moment before walking over. After a short pause, he answers, "Rain."

Okay… that's a start. "I see… a city in mist. The rain highlights its true beauty. A city in peace and quiet, unmarred by people or traffic." I tip my head back towards the table. "See my painting? I'm trying to capture that image and all of those things that I feel when I look at it."

"I don't see any of that," he says. "It's a mess out there. The sky has darkened, and there's no moon or stars to be seen. It's simply a shroud. What beauty is there to capture?"

"There's beauty in the night. Even without stars. Don't you get out?"

He glares haughtily at me. "Of course I get out! How else could I have gotten here?"

I chuckle. "I mean, don't you explore the city? Explore your world, explore life?"

Alexander hesitates. He turns away from the window. "My world is quite different from this one."

"How so?"

The side of his lip quirks up. "Did you really... how interesting." He looks around. "Are there any extra chairs?"

"Oh! Of course. I've been rude." I grab a stool from farther down the table and slide it next to mine. "Take a seat."

He settles in. "My world is... brighter. The colors are sharper, everything feels more alive. When you want something, you can have it at the blink of an eye. But at the same time... everything has been planned out for me. I need permission to explore."

"That sounds..." I hesitate. "I don't know, lonely. Kind of like a gilded cage."

"Exactly... like a gilded cage," he says in a low voice. Alexander sits next to me in silence for a while, sort of staring over my shoulder. I'm not quite sure what to do. Something is clearly troubling this man, but I don't know if I should try to get him to talk about it or let him simmer. And there's the little matter of trying to convince him of the value of great art.

Maybe... "Can I paint you?" I grab another smaller canvas on the other side of the table. "You have such an interesting face."

To my surprise, he shakes his head slowly. "Might I ask why?"

"Because..." I bite my lip awkwardly, "You have a handsome face. And I want to convince you a painting is much more than a decoration."

The room is quiet while he considers my request. I can practically see the gears in his head turning. Finally, he nods. "Okay. I'll let you give it a shot. Why not?"

Grinning, I switch out my city canvas for the blank one. Alexander leans over it a bit as I put it off to the side. "Perfect." As I pick up a piece of black chalk to sketch his features, I take a moment to inspect him closer. "You have the most striking blue eyes. Has anyone ever told you that? They're so bright."

He peers over at me in shock. I feel a rush of pride for that. He stares at me for a time before nodding. "No… not really."

"Well, I like them." My fingers work quickly, gliding the chalk across the page to capture the shape of Alexander's face before sketching out a few of his features. His eyebrows are high and arched over his deep-set eyes. His nose scoops upward slightly, which somehow really brings his face together. The tips of my fingers quickly get stained with black. "You have quite a long face. Very regal," I tease lightly. When I don't get a reaction, I wonder whether or not to apologize. *Not again!* In the end, I hold my tongue and begin to mix up Alexander's skin color. I make long brush strokes to cover the length of his face.

Out of the corner of my eye, I see Alexander lean forward to try to see what I'm creating. I shift forward so the canvas tips into his view. "So… What brings you to Lisden?"

"Life," he says quietly. "It's hard to explain." When I look up, he has a faraway look in his eye like he's recalling something he wants to forget.

"You don't have to explain," I reassure him. "Just smile." He raises an eyebrow, and I laugh lightly. "So I can paint your smile." He nods and gives me a slow smile. It's a soft smile, one that kind of creeps up on you and makes you smile too. I try to paint it just right with the smallest of brushes to get it right.

"And a little more blue…" I mumble to myself as I paint his eyes in. "And… there." I put the paintbrush down and spin the canvas around for Alexander to see. He looks at it quietly. His smile doesn't quite stay, but it doesn't fade either. I catch a glimpse of fascination in his eyes. *I'm winning.*

"Why?" His voice suddenly interrupts my internal celebration. "Why do you paint?"

That answer doesn't require much thought. "Because I love expressing the way I see the world through art. You can see how I feel through colors and brush strokes." I trail my fingers across the edge of the freshly painted canvas. "I can be heard without saying a word." I smile. "What do you think of the piece?"

"I don't know," he says. "It looks well made. But… I don't know. I'm having trouble seeing emotion in it."

I sigh. "You must think I'm crazy."

"No, not crazy. I'm just… still learning." He gives me another smile. *Maybe he's not beyond teaching after all.*

"Well, don't worry. There's a whole world out there to learn from."

He looks out the window to the rain that is beginning to shift from a downpour to a regular rainstorm. "Can I ask you something?"

"Sure."

"What piece of knowledge do you think to be the most valuable?" He turns back to me. "I can never find an answer that suits me. I have asked that question to scholars and children, men and women, but I can't find what I'm looking for. Something that holds true for me. What feels right."

I shift the canvas to lay across my lap as I consider the question. He's inquisitive, yet he misses the little things sometimes. It's like he needs someone to point them out for him to accept that they are there. "Well…" I finally start. "Finding who you are and what you believe in must be the most valuable piece of knowledge. It's the most powerful, isn't it? It's what we all long to find."

"Is it?" Alexander leans forward. "A child will tell you the location of his favorite candy store. A young boy will tell you the city he lives in. A laborer will tell you of a trick in his trade that has saved him the most time. But those things mean nothing to me. What need do I have for the tricks to a task I will never need?"

"No," I argue. "A child will tell you he's a dreamer. He wants to be an engineer or a soldier or a grocer. A young boy will tell you he's smart or kind or athletic. A laborer will tell you he works hard and values his family. Not what he knows. Who he is. The most important knowledge of a person is who they are and feel themselves to be."

He chuckles wryly. "Perhaps in your mind, they would answer like that, but you would be wrong in practice. A child would not know the implications of the question, only what things he knows have served him best. I've asked many people. They are selfish with what they know, at least in how they judge its worth." When he sees my somewhat confused expression, he shrugs sheepishly and finishes awkwardly, "Just something I think about."

"Is this what you do with your spare time?" I smile softly. "Contemplate the meaning of life."

"I have little else to do during my days."

"Little else?" I laugh lightly. "Why are you so cryptic?"

"I don't think it's so cryptic. I am rarely busy."

"That's wonderful. Lots of opportunity to explore then with all that time."

"Rather true."

I look around the room, which has gotten much dimmer as the sky has grown darker. Passing over the canvas to the young man, I get to my feet. "Looks like paint night is over. You keep this." I grab my jacket and slip it on. "I should get home..." As I say that, I see a hint of sadness in his eyes. I quickly add, "Unless... you want to grab a drink?"

Alexander looks out to the night sky and frowns slightly at the rain pouring down. For a moment, I think I've gone too far. But then he turns to look at me with a slight smile. "I think... some company would be nice."

I smile and grab my umbrella. "Come with me then. Hold this," I say as I practically shove it into his arms and quickly gather up my canvas and paints. "I know a cute cafe near here."

"That sounds nice," he says quietly.

I swing my bag over my shoulder. "Let us away then." When I open the studio door, Alexander fumbles with the umbrella. Once it's open, I take the man's arm and lead us down the path. "This way."

* * *

I take Alexander to a small cafe that stays open for late-night desserts and drinks. I introduce him to the guilty pleasure of chocolate lava cake, which he gratefully pronounces as his new favorite dessert. We chat idly late into the night about art and philosophy. He tells me about his favorite books that try to reason about the meaning of life, and I share my favorite artists and what kind of pieces they create. There's something refreshing about him and his perspective of life, and I can tell I'm slowly convincing him of art's importance in the world. But in the wee hours of the morning, he bids me good night and walks out the door. I never did find out where he is staying. By the time I thought to ask, he had vanished into the night. I wish I had asked him for contact information or where to find him while he's in town.

Life goes on, though. I usher myself home and get up early the next morning just like I always have for my job. I work weekdays at the local library sorting new arrivals and helping the kids find their next read. I love watching a young reader find the perfect book for the first time, the way their eyes light up as they sit in the big comfy chair and read.

The job also allows me to spend my late afternoons and evenings focusing on my art while I wait for someone to discover me. It's bound to happen sooner or later. In this city, one purchase from one of the high society men and women means a lifetime of making one's passion their career. There's an art show this weekend that promises to be another chance to get my work out there. I can't wait to go. I have been working for months on two pieces to showcase, and I'm hoping to make my break there.

Mid-week, during one particularly quiet afternoon, I spend time in the back shelving books. As I'm reaching up to put away a book on the highest shelf, a low voice interrupts me. "Hello again."

I whip around to find Alexander standing there. He smiles at me and takes the book from my hand, putting it in the empty space I was trying to reach.

I grin. "Hello to you too! Where did you come from?"

"I enjoy wandering through libraries, so I wanted to see what kind of books there were in town. Then I spotted you through the shelves and wanted to say hi."

"Well, isn't that just a wonderful coincidence?" I put away the other books in my arms. "How have you been enjoying your time in Lisden?"

Alexander leans against the shelf with his shoulder. "It's been fine. A little lonely." He hesitates. "I enjoyed your company a few nights ago."

"Really?" I internally dance. "I enjoyed it too. I'm really happy to see you."

He grins at me. "So… would you like to go out with me this weekend?"

I stare openly, and it takes all my self-control not to let my jaw drop as well. No man has asked me out in ages. When I was in secondary school, I had my fair share of boyfriends as the other girls did. But once I left, I didn't really get out to meet anyone, especially not mysterious, beautiful people like the man in front of me. "I… I would love to." Alexander's smile grows wider, which makes it so unfortunate that I must follow up with bad news. "But I have an art show this weekend. I have a table that I'm running."

"Oh… Well, that's alright. We can try again later in the—"

"Why don't you come with me?" I interrupt. "I would love to have company. We can get to know each other better. What do you think?"

"I think that sounds nice. Where should I meet you?"

"Downtown at the Galleria Hotel. It starts just before noon. Did you need directions?"

He shakes his head. "I'll figure it out." He gives me a little wave as he turns the corner away from me. "I'll see you there." As he walks away, I do a dance behind the bookcase. I get a few strange looks from some of the patrons, but I honestly don't care. I cannot wait to get closer to him. *Plus, another opportunity to teach him about art... What luck!* I laugh to myself before darting back to the circulation desk to finish out the day.

* * *

The Galleria Hotel is one of the most beautiful places in Lisden. It's an old, fine society hotel, towering to the sky with a big glass dome that sends light all the way down to the first floor. The first level is open, lobby and then conference space. That's where the art show is being held. When I walk inside the revolving doors, the lobby is milling with important people in fine gowns and suits chatting and drinking wine. I feel a bit out of place with my bag and my canvases, even in my best red dress. Rushing over to the sign-in table, I connect with the artist lead and move over to where my table is. Within a few minutes, I am placing my paintings on the various stands provided for me and lay out a few pieces on the table. Everything looks perfect.

"Amelia?" I hear a voice behind me. When I spin around, Alexander is standing there with a small smile.

"Hello! Welcome to the Galleria." I pull him over to the two chairs behind my table. "Come, sit with me. Did you just get here?"

"No, I've been here for a while. I thought I would look around first to see what all the fuss was about," he lightly teases.

"What did you find?"

He chuckles as he settles into his seat. "Colors. A lot of different types of pictures."

"What kinds?"

"Landscapes, still life, portraits. Anything you want, you could find here. There's other art here too. Sculptures, pottery. I'm a fan of clay."

"Really?" I ask. "So there is a type of art that you like."

"I like the movement in it, the idea of the hand manipulation involved to get the piece just right."

"There can be movement in paintings too, you know."

"You're right, there can be. I just haven't found one that speaks to me yet."

I nod thoughtfully. "I need to know more about you. What can you tell me?"

"I'm… smart," he finishes awkwardly. "I spend a lot of time in school and in training."

"What kind of training?"

He hesitates. "Politics."

My eyes widen. "You work for one of the city governments?"

"Yes."

"Which one?"

"If I told you, I'd have to take you in."

I groan loudly. "If you insist." I offer him my wrists. He chuckles and then takes my hands instead, tracing over the back of them lightly with his thumbs.

"I work with high profile people," he continues slowly with his eyes down at my hands. "I listen to their concerns and try to… come up with policy ideas based on what they need. It's very much a balancing act. Everybody needs something different from everyone else and finding something that takes care of the most people is difficult."

"That sounds fascinating. But complicated. Do you work with anyone on that?"

"I have a few… colleagues who I talk to and bounce ideas off of." Alexander runs a hand through his hair. "But other than that, it's usually up to me." He shakes his head. "But enough about me. Tell me something more about you. Like… your job. What made you want to work at the library?"

"Oh, I love books and working with people to find the right read," I answer energetically. "It's a place I have always wanted to work, and it's a great place to be at for the time being. I really love—"

"Miss?" A quiet voice interrupts me. I look up to see an older gentleman approaching my table. His white hair hangs down over the shoulders of his long black dress coat. His purple velvet tie stands out to me. *That's an expensive color.* I immediately straighten up my back and sit forward at my table.

"Yes, sir?" I reply.

"This piece over here…" He gestures to the small cityscape that I worked on the night I met Alexander. "When is this from?"

I flush in embarrassment. *I didn't mean for one of my quicker pieces to catch someone's eye like that! Maybe I should take it off the table.* "This is from this past week, sir. Just something I was trying out some new colors and practicing old techniques with. It's not one of my better works, but—"

To my surprise, he interrupts me. "Young lady, I think it is beautiful. And I would like to purchase it from you. In fact, I'd like to commission a larger piece for my estate. Is that something you would be interested in?"

I turn to Alexander in shock while he just grins at me. He motions for me to speak to the man, and I suddenly find my voice. "Yes, sir. I would absolutely be interested in that. May I have your information please?" A few moments later and I have more coins in my hand than I have seen in my lifetime for the painting and a deposit with a promise of more on the way after I complete the commission. When he leaves my table with a tip of his hat, I rush into Alexander's arms. He spins me around, and we laugh. "Did you see that?" I gush.

"Absolutely, look at you! What happens now?"

"I work on his commission as soon as possible, get exposure, hopefully gain some more projects. But until then…" I put my new coins into my bag and turn to him with a mischievous smirk. "Stay here with me until the event is over. Then go out with me and celebrate!" I grab his hand and squeeze it. "Won't you?"

His "yes" thrills me almost as much as gaining my first commission.

***

Alexander and I spend the evening out at a nice restaurant downtown before taking a midnight stroll through a park. I don't think I have ever enjoyed a night out more. Most dates wouldn't let me try a bite off of their plate, but Alexander was happy to share the fish he tried. He bought me a bouquet of lilies from a flower vendor about to take off for the night and passed them to me with a quirky flourish. When we reached the park, we must have talked for hours while the sky slowly changed from navy blue to a deep black. By the end of the night, we decide to continue experimenting with whatever this is between us.

The next week sweeps me off my feet. I go to work during the days and spend the rest of my time running around town with Alexander. We share a quick bite in the park during my lunch hour and idly talk about life and what we want from it. I share my dream about making my art my full-time job and starting a small family of my own. He talks about the pressures he has faced taking over the family business. How if he had the choice, he would do something different. Perhaps become a teacher. I think it's a noble goal and one that suits him well. We have a picnic on the hilltop just outside the city at twilight. I try to sear it in my memory so I can paint it later.

Alexander makes me feel fulfilled. Like my life doesn't move from home to work and back home again. He gives me something to look for and even hope for… a future. I don't know where the two of us are going, but I want to keep going down this path. But when Alexander meets me again for lunch, his face is much more solemn.

"What's wrong?" I ask.

He stays silent for a while before answering flatly. "I have to leave town tonight,"

My head turns swiftly to him. "So soon?"

"I'm sorry," he murmurs before turning away.

I hate to see him look so sad, so I nudge his shoulder with mine. "That's alright. You'll be in town again soon, won't you?"

The look in his eyes causes my heart to sink into my stomach. "I… am due to take my father's place at… the family workplace. Once I am installed there, I will never be able to make it out this way again."

"Surely not never?" My voice goes up a bit in pitch. "Surely, I'll see you again."

He smiles gently and brushes his knuckles lightly against my cheek. "I highly doubt our paths will cross again."

"I could come with you—"

"Amelia." Alexander puts his hands on my shoulders. "My life at home is so vastly different from this one. I live very far away, and you have a life here. A good one. You have dreams to live and work in this city."

I shake my head. "I can paint anywhere."

"Amelia." His voice grows softer. I see in his eyes that he is trying not to say that this is the end of our dalliance, but I can read him plain as day. He may not be willing to take me to his home for perfectly legitimate reasons, but it seems that even if he could, he doesn't seem to want to continue this relationship. But my heart just isn't quite ready to let him go.

"One more night?" I ask. When he turns his head away with a chuckle, I force it back to look at me. "One more night in town. Stay for one more night, please. Let me take you out on one last hurrah."

"I'm sorry, Amelia, but I have really got to get back."

"Please." I turn my best set of pleading eyes towards him.

He considers the idea for a while. Behind his eyes, I can see the thoughts turning. Finally, to my delight, he nods once. "Alright. One more night. Where shall we go?"

I take his arm. "I have just the place. Dress nice and meet me at my apartment at dinner. I'll make us something." In a moment of spontaneity, I rise on my toes, kiss him on the cheek, and rush off down the street. When I peek over my shoulder, I spot his shocked, yet bemused expression. A sneaky smile crosses my face before I round the corner and rush home.

My apartment is a small one-bedroom apartment on the upper floors of the Balia Complex only a few blocks away from the heart of downtown. It costs a pretty copper, but the location couldn't be more perfect. I like being in the thick of things. When I arrive home, I set straight away to straighten things up. It's amazing how quickly such a small place can get so messy. I have got to get everything together, go grocery shopping, and sort out an itinerary in a few short hours.

If tonight is really to be Alexander's last night in town, then the only thing I can do is make it a night that he will remember.

* * *

A knock comes at the door around sundown. I quickly hang up my apron and straighten the bottom of my blue dress. Fluffing my hair over my shoulders, I open my door with a smile. Alexander stands there in a smart blue button-down shirt and black pants with this perfectly messy hair that I absolutely adore.

"Hello," I say as I bite my lip.

"Hello," he says in a low tone, smiling at me. "You look lovely."

"Thank you." I open the door wider and step aside. "Come in." He steps through the door into my living room and looks around the place. I trail behind him anxiously. "Welcome to my little home."

"It's really nice," he muses as he turns around to look at me. "It looks like I thought it would."

"And how is that?"

"Bright. Colorful. Comfortable."

I beam at the compliment. "Thanks. I've been living here for a few years now, and I do my best to make it feel homey."

Alexander sits down on my red couch. "Something smells great."

"Yes, I made pasta with meatballs, and there's a cherry pie in the oven." I move over to the stovetop to check on the boiling pot. "This should be ready in just a minute, if you'll set the table. Plates are in the top left cabinet, and silverware is in the bottom drawer."

Alexander moves somewhat hesitantly from the couch into the kitchen, but then quickly gets to pulling dishes out and getting them arranged. I dump the pasta into my strainer and pull the meatballs from the oven. After serving both of us, I take my seat at the head of the table. He sits down across from me.

The apartment is silent while we dig in. Every so often, I glance up to see Alexander looking at me. But every time I raise my head to meet his eyes, he looks back down. We go through about five rounds of that before I finally put my fork down and say, "Is this awkward to you?"

A rush of relief runs across his face. "So much. I'm sorry, I haven't really been on a "last date" before; I have no idea what to say to you."

I laugh lightly. "That's okay. You don't have to know. We can just… talk. About anything. It doesn't have to be some significant thing. It can be random like… what color are your favorite pair of shoes?"

Alexander lets out a short laugh. "Silver."

"Silver?"

"My favorite pair of slippers," he says nonchalantly before taking another bite.

I have a tiny fit of giggles. "My favorite pair of shoes… is red. I feel very powerful in red shoes."

"Why red?"

"I don't know. It reminds me of my grandma, I guess." I smile softly at the memory. "She always wore this beautiful red scarf to every visit. It smelled like peppermint tea. That was my grandmother's favorite tea. She taught me how to paint."

"Really?"

"Yes. She was an amazing artist, a thousand times better than me. She created the most beautiful landscapes, particularly of the beach. She lived down by the coast."

"Lived?"

"Yeah…" I sigh. "My grandmother passed a couple years ago."

"I'm sorry to hear that."

"Thank you. I try to keep her memory alive by continuing on with my art and wearing something red every so often when I want her strength to flow through me."

"That sounds really nice." Alexander looks somewhere off over my shoulder. "Who is that in the picture over there?" He motions to the tiny shelf I have hanging by the door where sits a picture of me and a baby boy with a cute blue hat. "Is that your brother or cousin?"

I inwardly cringe and close my eyes tightly, putting my fork down. "I… I should have told you."

"What is it?" He looks so confused, and my stuttering isn't making matters much clearer.

"That's my son," I blurt out. Alexander's fork clunks loudly against the side of the plate as it slips out of his hand. I roll quickly into my next words, trying to take up the uncomfortable silence. "I know I should have told you last week, but I could never find the right time to say something on any of our dates; we've never talked about family before and then you said you were leaving tomorrow—"

"Amelia," Alexander interrupts me. "It's okay."

I stop mid-sentence. "What?"

"It's okay. I don't mind that you have a kid. Sure, I might have liked to know earlier so maybe I could have met him. But… I don't blame you for not saying something."

A wash of relief rolls over my shoulders as I pick up my fork again and continue to eat. "Wow… well… thank you."

"What's his name?"

"Leo."

"Where is he?"

"He's at my mom's. She watches him three nights a week for me so I can take care of the house and do my art. I've tried to pay her a hundred times, but she won't accept my money. She likes the time with her grandchild."

"And the father?"

I gulp softly. "Gone."

"I'm sorry," he quickly apologizes. "I didn't mean to—"

I wave him off. "Don't worry about it." I get to my feet and head over to the oven. "Why don't we try dessert and you tell me about your favorite… musical instrument."

"Oh, now that's tough," he chuckles as he grabs two small plates out of my cabinet. The conversation evolves slowly as we dig into dessert. When the pie tin is half empty, I put it away in my fridge, and we leave the apartment together. I lead him through the alleyways until we come to my decided destination for the night, a small hole-in-the-wall club called Pan's Underground.

"I think you'll like this place," I say as I push open the door quickly. The flashing lights skim over us as we get settled into the heavy beat of the music. Beautiful people in all arrays of black and white suits and dresses with bright ties and sashes dance in the middle of the floor. The bartender slides drinks to patrons down the bar counter on the right side of the room. Everything about this place is high, intense energy. It beckons me closer.

"Woah," I hear him breathe beside me. I grin and pull him over to the dance floor. Turns out Alexander is a fantastic dancer, and we spend the whole night lost in the music. We don't leave until the club owners are practically forcing everyone out of the door. We race home, laughing.

When we reach my apartment door, I fumble for my keys. "Here we are. Back home." I turn around to give Alexander a smile but find his face to be right up next to mine. I didn't expect him to be so close. He looks at me with an unfamiliar gaze. I look from his eyes down to his lips and then back up. There's a tension between us. It's been there all night.

Which way, I'm not sure. I don't know whether to step forward or step back. Our heads lean closer together until my forehead rests against his lightly. His lips catch mine in a soft kiss. The dam breaks, and I can't tear myself away from him.

My keys slip out of my hand and hit the ground as I throw my arms around his neck. His kiss is gentle, but growing more insistent as we tumble into each other. He breaks the kiss to grab my keys and press them into my hands. Pushing them into the lock and spinning the knob, we rush into my apartment.

Everything moves fast from there. Alexander's kisses grow deeper and more passionate, and I grip him closer. It isn't long until our clothes are scattered across my floor all the way to the bedroom. I fall more in love with every touch of his hand on my body, every kiss laid on my skin. At the end of the night, I tumble down into the man's arms and pray to the Lady never to leave again.

* * *

When I wake in the morning, I feel a coolness that was not there when I fell asleep. I roll over to find that Alexander is not there. The sleepiness in my eyes fades almost immediately as I jerk upright. The man's clothes are gone, and everything in the room that we upset overnight has made its way back to where it came from. Even the empty pillow beside me seems to have been fluffed and straightened.

If I wasn't still feeling the effects of last night, I would have wondered if I had dreamed the whole thing. We did have quite a bit to drink.

I push the covers off of me fully and slip my slippers on. That's when I spot the small card on the table with my name on the front. When I pick it up and turn it over to the other side, my heart sinks. All it says is, *Thank you for the best time I have had in a long time. Good luck with everything; I hope you find everything you want in life. I wish you only the best. I won't forget you, Amelia.*

Slamming the card onto the desk, my heart just pounds into my chest. How dare he leave without saying goodbye? How dare he leave me a note and… I groan and sniffle when I see the purple lily next to it. Such an unfitting and yet heartbreaking exit. I try to explain it, justify it to myself. Maybe he had an early train; maybe he received an urgent communication and he had to rush home. *But then why wouldn't he wake me up?*

I sit back down on the edge of the bed, and I stay there for a long time. My thoughts race. Part of me wants to forget that any of this ever happened. But remembering that soft smile and the feeling of his lips against my skin is too raw, too… real. When I think about it longer, there is nothing I truly want to forget. Although he disappeared without a proper goodbye, I imagine he left before he was unable to leave me. It breaks my heart, but I understand it.

It wasn't until many weeks later that I realized I would never be able to quite put him out of mind. When I started feeling nauseous almost every morning, I took myself to the doctor. Come to find out, I was pregnant with Alexander's child. Nine months later, when my baby Grace opened her eyes and had the same bright blue ones that my Alexander had, I knew that she would have the same spark he did. With a little luck, I would be able to help her find it too.

II

Taking My Place

Elise's Story

II

Whenever Daddy goes to work at the palace, he never brings me. He says I'm too loud and will cause him too much trouble. Even when I beg him to take me, he doesn't listen. He pats me on the head and leaves. When Mama died though, he couldn't find a nanny in time for his next meeting, and so he had no choice but to take me.

"Elise," he said to me, "when we get to the palace, I will leave you with a servant. You will stand still and not make any trouble, and if you do, I will take you into town for a treat." The promise of sweets kept me quiet as our carriage pulled up to the courtyard.

The palace of the House of the Evening is so pretty. It's big and purple and glittery; I really want to explore. But Daddy doesn't even let me look up at it for too long before he takes my hand and drags me forward into the front hall. There is an old lady waiting by the staircase with gray hair and an apron. She smiles at my father like she knew we were coming. Daddy brings me over and starts talking to her, but I don't pay attention. I'm too busy looking at my reflection on the floor. It's so shiny, it's like a mirror.

Daddy tugs my arm. "Sweetheart, I need you to wait with Amy here while I speak to someone, alright?" He looks at me with that serious look he gives me when he wants me to behave. "Stand here with her. Do not run off." After leaning down and kissing my head, he leaves the hall to speak to a man in the other room with the big chairs.

I peer around the corner as far as I can lean. It might be the throne room. I want to see inside more, but every time I try to take a tiny step forward, the old woman clears her throat and gives me a stern look like Daddy. I don't like it very much at all. I shuffle my feet and look up at the tall ceiling where the sun is shining in from the circle windows.

I hear a small sound like a giggle, and I whip around to see a little boy peeking around the corner of the hallway. He has brown hair and really bright blue eyes. When I stare at him, he slowly comes out from behind the wall before rushing to where I'm standing. He gives me a big grin before speaking in a deep voice "Hello." The voice doesn't sound right, and I laugh at him. The old woman clears her throat again, louder this time, but the boy speaks again before I get to look at her. This time, in a normal voice. "I'm Alexander. Who are you?"

"I'm Elise," I smile at him. "Do you live here?"

He puffs up his chest. "I do! I'm the High Lord!"

I giggle. "You're too small to be the High Lord." The old woman shushes me with a mean scowl, and I stare at her. "What?"

The boy slumps slightly and pouts. "But I ammmm. I am Alexander Faelie!"

My eyes grow big. *I remember that name!* "Are you Lord Alexander?"

He grins. "Yep!"

I gasp. I've never met a Lord before. "That's amazing! You must have so much fun here. You can do whatever you want!"

To my surprise, he frowns. "I wish..." he whines. "I have to do what everyone tells me as I grow up."

I frown too. "That's terrible." I look around the big empty front hall, and I suddenly get an idea. Looking sideways at the old lady to make sure she doesn't hear me, I whisper loudly to Alexander. "For now, you get to play though... right?"

"Yeah..." the boy answers slowly.

"Do you play tag?"

"Tag? What's that?"

My mouth falls open. *How does a Lord not know what tag is?* "It's a game!" I shout. "We chase each other around and tag each other with a hand to change who chases who. It's tag!"

"Why would we chase each other?"

"For fun! It's a game."

Alexander looks confused. "But… how is chasing fun?"

"It just is!" I throw my hands up dramatically. "I could show you." He looks over at the woman behind me and frowns. I whisper again, "We could ditch her."

He stares at me in shock. "What?! We could never."

"We're fast! Aren't you fast?"

"Yeah… but why?"

"I'm bored," I whine.

"We can't just leave."

"Why not?"

"It's wrong!"

I shrug. "Fine… if you say so." Out of the corner of my eye, I see my father walking back towards me. I run over to him and take his hand. "I have to go now. But… it was nice to meet you!" Daddy has a strange look on his face, kind of like how he looks when I surprise him with a birthday present but bigger. "Maybe I can come again and visit sometime." My dad rushes us out the door before I can even hear an answer! But I do see Alexander waving wildly at me as I leave, so I wave back just as big.

I wonder if I'll see him again.

* * *

It wasn't until I was thirteen that I got to return to the palace again. This time, I was invited as a guest to the teen Lord's birthday. It was an honor to be one of those selected, handpicked out the children of officials close to the palace. My father is one of the mid-ranking officials, not an automatic choice, but close enough to work reasonably often with those in the palace. Lord Alexander was turning fourteen, the age where a noble heir begins the final stage of their ascension to the throne. His birthday is a milestone for the House of the Evening and a sign of what is to come.

I'm not quite at the age where I have to be prim and proper all the time as the mark of an official's daughter, but I'm supposed to look nice at these kinds of events. Though regarding the invitation, I have no idea what to expect. The invitation references some sort of garden party, but I can't fathom why the lord heir would be a fan of one of those. Who knows, maybe it's tradition, and I'm just ignorant. My father has my nanny take me out to buy a new dress, something pale and purple that rests just above my knees.

It's times like these I really miss my mother. I wish she was here to take me out to buy dresses for my first dances and teach me how to talk to boys without feeling awkward. I miss her presence. I can barely remember her now. Only flashes and glimpses of a gentle face and a warm hug. My father says he sees her in me. But that doesn't really make me feel better.

"Elise, dear," my father calls from the front hall. "Your carriage is here." I slip my shoes on and rush downstairs. My father gives me a soft smile. "You look wonderful."

"Dad," I flush in embarrassment.

"You do," he protests. "Can't a father compliment his daughter? Do you have your gift?"

"It should be on the table." I suddenly remember. Rushing to the dining room, I grab the yellow wrapped package and rush back to the door. "I have to go, I don't want to be late."

"Have a good time," my father says as he kisses the top of my head. I give him a quick hug before dashing down the front steps to the coach. The driver helps me up inside and closes the door behind me. Within a few moments, we take off for the castle.

Riding down the streets of Silvervale, the main town, in an actual carriage is a magical experience. The people we pass raise on their toes to peer through the window to see who is riding by in such transport. I love the feeling of the cobblestone under the wheels, giving the carriage a little bounce. As we get closer to the palace, I nitpick at my dress and my hair, smoothing a bit here and tucking a bit there. When I walk into the palace, I want to make a good impression. The noble family's influence is far-reaching, and a kind word or the right movement could catch the eye of some important people in my future.

As we approach the palace, we meet other carriages ascending the winding hill. My carriage falls in line. My heart pounds in my chest as I peer out the window and see the familiar purple hue of the castle exterior. *What a sight.* The towers rise up to the sun and glisten softly in the light. My favorite parts are the big balconies that stretch out so the nobles can look at the entire House below. I wonder what it would be like to stand up there and see the world you governed. It must feel so powerful.

The carriage finally rolls to a stop in the courtyard once it can get close enough to the offloading place. The driver hops down and swings open my door. "Enjoy the party, miss.," he says to me with a small nod. "I will return for you when it is over." I climb out of the vehicle and give a small curtsy to the driver. Then squaring my shoulders, I follow a handful of other kids into the palace. We are greeted by a handful of maids who take shawls and dress jackets and direct us through the hallway to the back.

Through the back double doors, we move into a huge open field where chaos erupts. There's a group of boys wrestling and rolling down a hill in the back, another group of kids chasing each other, and a group of girls sitting over at a few tables eating pastries and laughing. I recognize my friend, Bethany. She gives me a little wave, and I separate from the group, making my way over to her quickly. "Beth, it's so good to see you!" I embrace her.

"Oh, Elise, it's been so long. How have you been?"

"I'm doing alright." I take her hands as we sit down next to each other. "What a party, huh?"

"You don't know the half of it. It's only been a little while, and Lord Alexander has already taken down half of the officials' sons in their impromptu wrestling match. He's been boasting loudly about his athletic prowess. If he wasn't the future High Lord… oof… someone needs to give him a piece of their mind."

I laugh. "Beth, you think every boy who brags for two seconds should get a talking to."

She shrugs. "What can I say? Men are idiots."

As the party goes on, Beth and I chat and idly munch on some fruit tarts. Eventually, the group of wrestling boys breaks apart, and Lord Alexander steps out towards the middle of the field. He's grown up quite a bit. He's turned into a tall, sort of gangly boy with this brilliant, sort of arrogant smile. He strides closer to the main group and says, "Hey! I bet anyone here the first slice of birthday cake that nobody… can outshoot me in archery."

There's a soft chuckle that kind of resonates throughout the party, but no one really knows how to answer him. *Is it proper to challenge the Lord? Is it proper if he asks for the challenge?* "Any takers?" No one says a word. All the side conversations even fall silent. "No one?"

Out of the corner of my eye, I see Beth's eyes shift. I immediately clamp down on her hand. "Don't do it," I hiss.

But it's too late. She stands up and grabs my arm, dragging me up with her. The embarrassment is super evident on my face. "Elise might be able to!" she calls to the Lord. "She's the best shooter I know here."

"Beth!" I whisper. "What are you doing?"

Unfortunately, the young Lord heard her. "Elise, get out here," he calls out to me. Inwardly cursing my best friend's name, I trudge over to him. With a wave of the Lord's hand, servants quickly set up a handful of targets across the big field. The two of us are handed a set of arrows and a decent bow. Lord Alexander looks over at me with a cocky grin. "Are you sure you want to go up against me?"

"Absolutely." I roll my eyes and test the tightness of the bowstring.

"Alright, if you say so." *Beth was right; his condescension is getting old fast.* With a sideways glance over to me, he raises the bow and shoots. The arrow flies and hits the edge of the bullseye. He cheers loudly before firing off another four arrows in quick succession. Each one lands in approximately the same general area on the targets. *He's not bad, I'll give him that.* The crowd around us applauds his efforts.

Then it's my turn.

I get the bow into position and take a breath before letting the string fly. The first arrow hits the target just right of Alexander's, closer to the center. A murmur echoes through the crowd. The Lord looks appalled. Going a bit slower than he did, I let my next four arrows fly methodically, placing them in similar positions. When the last one smacks the dead center of the bullseye, I can't help but grin.

"What the hell?" The Lord's voice says behind me. I turn to see him right up in my face. "How the hell did you do that?"

"I've been doing archery since I was seven years old. It's one of my father's favorite sports. He made sure I knew what I was doing with a bow and arrow."

"I demand a rematch!"

"Well, I think it's clear who won here." I laugh lightly.

To my surprise, he pushes me backward with both hands. I stumble back and barely catch myself. "Another round," he says again, this time more forcefully.

"Don't push me!" I shout. "Just because you aren't as good as you think you are doesn't mean I should purposefully miss to make you feel better!"

"Who do you think you are?!"

"Who do you think *you* are?!"

"I'm the Lord of this castle, and I want you to get out!"

In a blur, I lunge at him in a blind rage. His eyes widen as I land on top of him. Suddenly, the two of us are wrestling in the grass, tearing clothes and scratching. I feel the bottom hem of my dress tear, and I know I ripped a button out of his shirt. The kids around us are just cheering wildly and shouting, "Fight! Fight! Fight!"

We roll around and nearly take out a few girls at the shins. Eventually, two of the servants pull us apart.

I look at the Lord, breathing heavily. He looks completely disheveled. Shirt collar sideways, pants torn at the bottom, and his hair. By the Lady, his hair is sticking out in all directions. He looks like he has been struck by lightning. I imagine I don't look much better. The incredulity of the situation bubbles up inside of me, and I burst out laughing. Everyone is staring at me, but I don't care. I double over as I lose myself in giggles.

After a while, the Lord's confused eyes start to twitch. Then he starts chuckling too. The servants let go of the two of us cautiously as we both dissolve into outright loud and proud laughter. "My Lord," I finally manage to choke out. "I am… so… I…"

"Miss Elise, I don't…" He laughs. "I don't know what that was."

The group around us starts to laugh as well, smaller laughs, more polite. Lord Alexander and I move towards each other and shake hands. "Why don't we try some of that cake?" he offers.

"Why not?" I giggle, and we make our way over to the cake table, followed by a group of hungry preteens and teenagers. The rest of the party goes off without a hitch, and as far as I know, none of the servants ever snitched on us to the noble family. Or maybe they did. I guess

I'll find out when I try to take advantage of opportunities in the future. *Attacking the future High Lord is probably not the best look.*

* * *

I love manipulating the wind. It's tempestuous, relentless, and uncontrollable at the best of times, and I love being the one to tame it. When I first started out, I got carried away with every mild breeze. Now, I can bend storms to my will. I may not have a lot of affinities, but the ones I do have, I have taken the time to hone with my tutor, Marcus. Since I was seven years old, all I wanted to do was learn magic. It gave me such a thrilling feeling to not just know that I had these amazing powers, but also to learn to understand them.

One afternoon, I sit underneath the big oak tree behind the house and play around with the breeze. When I feel it brush through my hair, I catch it in my hand. The wind fights against me, but I hold fast. Swirling it tight from a strand into a ball, I balance it in my hands. I bounce it back and forth from side to side before unraveling it into a string again. My magic slowly lengthens it out until I can crack the wind like a whip. With each act, the wind fights me. I don't let it escape.

"Elise!" My father calls me from the back door of our home. "I need to speak to you in my office. Now!"

Surprised slightly at the firmness of his tone, I let the wind out into the world again and rush over to the house. I brush a couple of leaves out of my hair and straighten myself before walking into my father's office. He sits in his tall desk chair with his hands folded on the desk. "What is it, Father?"

He smiles warmly and puts me at ease. "I wanted to talk to you about your future." My heart pounds quickly. *It's finally time.* I quickly take a seat in the chair set up opposite him. "I have been incredibly pleased with your progress in your education. Your skill with wind magic is second only to the High Lord himself, and you have consistent top marks in your general education work. And your private lessons?"

"They have been going well. Master Florian says my flute playing has improved. Would you like me to play for you?"

He waves my offer off with a hand. "I don't need a demonstration right now. What I want to know is… Have you given any consideration to the type of match you want to make? I know you have aspirations of your own, darling, but a fruitful marriage could afford you those luxuries. Being a wife of some of these officials or high-ranking soldiers would mean a variety of opportunities that you can't afford on my salary and an abundance of connections."

"I have no interest in being a soldier's wife, Father," I half groan. "I don't want to be dragged to every formal event in the House; I want to be hosting them. I want to be driving cultural change, the woman that other girls look up to."

"That makes me wonder if you already know what you want to do."

I smile softly. "I do." I take a deep breath. "I want you to get me into the running for the next High Lord's wife."

My father is taken aback. His eyes widen imperceptibly, and his mouth keeps forming words that his voice just won't say. After a while, he finally blurts out, "Excuse me?"

I can't help but chuckle a little. "You heard me. I want to be in the pool for Lord Alexander's wife."

"The High Lord considers only the most prestigious of women. Sometimes noble, often wealthy or with some kind of incredible ability. My child, you don't fall into any of those. I work with the High Lord occasionally, but I am very low tier compared to others. How do you expect to compete?"

"That's on me, Dad," I say firmly. "You get me the invite, and I will take it from there."

He looks at me for a long time with an unreadable expression. Then he simply nods once and gets to his feet. "Alright. Don't get your hopes up, though. It won't be easy."

"I don't mind." I keep myself from grinning too broadly, instead turning away and walking back outside. What my father doesn't realize is that I plan to take the High Ladyship by any and all means necessary.

* * *

When I enter the palace's throne room for the first time, I am admittedly nervous. My red dress brushes against the tile floor as the sound of my voice being announced echoes through the room. As I make my way over to where the High Lord and his family are sitting, I keep my head high and my shoulders back. Every move I make in this room will be judged with an impeccable eye. Multiple eyes. I must be perfect. Two other young women, Alandra Riesland and Cassandra Tamlin wait in the middle of the floor. They are the others chosen to be presented to Lord Alexander, soon to be High Lord of the House of the Evening. I take my place on the far right of them.

My father was able to get me into the pool of potential matches for the High Lord by calling in every favor he had. One person spoke to another who worked with someone else who knew another who placed me on the list. I and two dozen other women were invited to one of the High Lady's winter homes for a conference of sorts. From there, the real fun began.

We were tested in magic, intellect, and general poise. Although my powers aren't as vast as my competitors, I cast circles around a few. My wind magic was one of the most stunning displays there, according to the High Lady. But frankly, I didn't exactly leave it up to chance. Fire could be blown out in a quiet breeze, and balancing acts could be derailed. Wind is one of those subtle elements that is often present on chaotic days or bright ones. It is so easy to slip a little breeze in and not get caught. In the library, the High Lady's personal housekeeper quizzed us on realm history and basic literature. To me, I feel like there should have been more questions on diplomacy or how to run a realm's finances, but maybe the High Lady isn't involved in that. Perhaps she should be.

I cut whatever corners I can on my way to the top, sabotaging dresses and sending gusts to trip girls on their way down the stairs. No injuries, I'm not that devious. But I just knew I had to make it to the top three. Once I made it to the palace… then I could speak to Lord Alexander directly.

The High Lord's voice interrupts my thoughts. "The three of you young ladies have proven yourselves to be worthy matches for my son. He will be choosing his bride from the three of you. You will each have a few minutes to speak to him. Make them count. He then stands up and waves for Cassandra and me to step out of the throne room. We wait outside in the hallway silently while the High Lord and High Lady talk in hushed tones to each other. After a few minutes, Alandra steps out of the room, and Cassandra goes in. She takes longer than the girl before her. All the while, I stand there with my head down and my hands clutched in front of my body. My stomach is in knots.

When Cassandra steps out and waves me in, I take a deep breath and stride purposefully towards the door. As it shuts behind me, I look up to see Lord Alexander sitting on his throne with a slightly bored expression on his face. He stands up to greet me as he comes in like he's been programmed to do so, but he pauses when he looks up at me. "Elise?"

I smile softly. "Hello, Lord Alexander." I dip softly into a curtsy.

"I remember you…" He studies me for a minute, walking around me. "My fourteenth birthday. We argued." I grimace and resist the urge to swear. *I was hoping he didn't remember that.* "That was you, wasn't it?"

I sigh. "Yes. That was me."

II

To my surprise, the Lord laughs. "You had a strong will then. Do you still have one?"

"Yes."

"And you think that's what I want in a woman?" He raises an eyebrow. I can tell that he's being playful, but he also is genuinely curious about the question.

I think about it for a while. "Yes," I finally answer. "You want someone with a strong will. And… someone who listens to you too. Doesn't run over with her thoughts. At the same time, she can… take control of a room. Give you advice about what you need to do next."

"And you think that's you?"

"I hope so."

Alexander looks flustered. "Look, can I be honest with you?" I nod quickly. "I hate this. I don't think it's fair for me to have to decide what kind of woman I want in only a day. What kind of system is this?"

"I agree. I think it's a little old-fashioned."

"I don't want this for my kids."

"Neither would I."

He looks at me carefully. "Out of the women here, you seem the least abhorrent. I've seen you before, we've chatted. Argued. I don't think I could ever get bored with you. How about a deal?"

I try not to hide the growing sense of victory in my chest. "What kind of deal?"

"Agree to be my bride. Tell my father you want a long engagement. We get to know each other slowly. Go out a few times. Talk. If I like you, we'll be married. If not, I'll set you up with whatever opportunities you wish to undertake, the best that money can buy, in exchange for you walking away. What do you think of that?"

I pretend to think about it for a while. Then I hold my hand out to shake. "I would say you have yourself a deal, Lord Alexander."

He smiles and shakes it firmly. Placing his hand on my back and taking my hand, he guides me towards the door. "Let's tell my parents, shall we?"

***

"High Lady, I need you to give me one more push," the physician says just beyond the ringing in my ears. "One more push. Take a breath. One… two… three!" I scream and squeeze Alexander's hand as tightly as I can. When I hear my baby's cry for the first time, I can't help but burst into tears as I slump back into the pillow. For so long, I have been hoping to make a family of my own. And finally, with my High Lord at my side, I have that dream.

"Congratulations, High Lord, High Lady. It's a boy." The physician places the crying, freshly spelled clean child into my arms, and I hold him close to my chest. I hush him urgently as I look down at him, and slowly but surely, he starts to quiet. When his little blue eyes look up at me, as brilliant as my husband's, my heart just falls. He is the most precious being I have ever laid eyes on. He would be my greatest treasure.

Alexander brushes his hand over the baby's head with reverence. There's a brightness in his eyes that makes me fall in love with him even more. "He's so small," he breathes.

"He's perfect," I answer quietly as I hold the child closer.

"Have you thought of a name yet?" The physician asks as he heads for the door to give us some privacy.

"Yes," I answer quietly as I rub my baby's little hand. "Neil Sonra Faelie. Neil after his father and Sonra after mine."

"That's a perfect name."

"Yes, it is…" Alexander smiles as he slides in closer to my side to hold me and our child. As the physician leaves us and I settle back into my husband, I feel this urge deep inside of me to be strong for this child.

To be the mother I never had to him. Looking at him, I make a silent vow to always put him first, to lift him up whenever he needs my help, and to never let anything happen to him.

After all, my child is to be the heir to the House of the Evening. He is destined to be someone incredible, and I am going to be by his side when he discovers who that is.

III

Coming To Terms

Neil's Story

Author's Note: This story contains major spoilers for Chasing Fae. Read at your own risk.

III

For my entire life, I have been the chosen one.

As the sole heir to the House of the Evening, it has always been expected of me to perform well in everything I do. In intellect, in magical skill, and in political policy, I must stand out among those who came before me. I was born into this life, and I fit into it perfectly. No expense was spared for my education and my magical training, and I have spent the last couple of years at my father's side, learning politics and diplomacy as he executed it. But as I approach the day that I am poised to take over the High Lordship, I wonder if I have what it takes. Father says that that feeling is common to have as the administration changes, so I try not to worry too much. I still have a long way to go before the torch is passed.

When the High Lord is gone on official business, things are exceptionally quiet around the palace. Without him around to keep me engaged in the daily workings of noble life, I'm bored. There's only so much time one can spend pouring over legal documents and practicing magical fundamentals before they start to go crazy. The family and I should have gone with him to the Winter Solstice celebration in the House of the Sun, but Mom got sick and Father thought it would be best for her to rest. So he went alone, and we stayed to celebrate a quiet Solstice at the palace.

Though I did get to dive into action once during the holiday. Two trading ships down at the docks collided when heavy winds brought them too close together. One ship from the House of Water lost most of its cargo while another from the House of Wind skated by with only a few losses. The House of Water blamed the House of Wind for the collision, and a fight broke out at the docks. When my father's right-hand man rushed down to oversee the situation with some of the other officials, I went with them. We took a representative from each ship and testimony from witnesses on the water and eventually reached an amicable resolution. We were able to chalk it up to the storm, and although the sailors went home empty-handed, we didn't start an inter-House incident. A spark of pride bloomed within me from helping to solve a problem without my father's instruction.

Luckily, my overall boredom should end soon. My father is due home today from the festivities. Finally, things can get back to normal around here. But there's something different in the air. There has been an odd energy around the palace all day. No matter which room I walk into, whispers echo. Even my little sister, Analise, has noticed it. Every time my mother or I walk into a room, there's an odd look in the servants' eyes. Like they know something they are not supposed to know. Granted, they are usually more into the know than the nobles and officials are a lot of the time. My father often will ask around if there's an issue he is trying to sort out to see if anyone has any useful information. I would ask, but they aren't sticking around long enough for me to try. I'm tired of walking into a room and having people scatter. It gives me this uncanny feeling like there's something big coming and I'm the only one left out of the loop.

As soon as breakfast is over, I meet my mother in the throne room to greet him. To my surprise, her expression is troubled rather than excited. She holds a letter in her hand.

"Mother?" I ask quietly. Her head swings up to look at me quickly. "Are you alright?"

Her lips curl into a soft smile as she tucks the letter into her sleeve. "Yes, my child, I'm fine. Just reading a note from your father."

"Will he still be coming home today?"

"Yes, but… he wants us to convene in this room rather than meet him in the courtyard."

My brow furrows. "Did he give a reason as to why? Is everything alright?"

"I'm not sure," she says. "He said he would explain when he arrived." She motions me over to her. "Have a seat, Neil. It won't be much longer now." I take my place on the throne next to her and lean back into it a bit. "Have you seen your sister?"

"Not yet. Though I expect we'll hear her in a minute." Sure enough, within the next couple moments, little footsteps can be heard clomping down the stairs. I suppress a chuckle. Analise hasn't mastered the noble dignified walk yet. She pretty much runs and clomps around wherever she goes. She rushes in and leaps into my mom's lap.

"Dad's coming home today!" She beams. "When is he coming, Mom?"

"Soon, darling, we have to be patient." Mom smiles down at the girl.

"It's been ages though," she groans. "I wanted to go to the party."

"We had a nice Solstice at home, didn't we?" Mom lightly chastises her. "We took a nice carriage ride through town and had a nice dinner. That wonderful flautist played for us. Remember?" My sister eventually nods in agreement. "And we'll celebrate with your father when he comes home."

The soft rumble of carriage wheels echoes through the lobby into the throne room, and all of us sit up a little to listen closer. The caravan is arriving. There's an instant shift in the air. This heavy anticipatory atmosphere changes to a rush of energy. Analise bounces incessantly on her toes and rocks her body back and forth. If I was younger, I likely would have done the same thing.

The doors to the palace open, and I hear a few pairs of footsteps make their way inside. I am tempted to move to the doorway to meet him, but his instructions to wait were quite clear. I wonder and even worry a bit over what kind of news he has for us. It has to be something significant; he never makes us wait when he's been away for a while. I worry there's a diplomatic dispute or something similar that has made him uneasy. But even then, *why would he stop us from greeting him?*

When Father walks into the throne room, Analise leaps into his arms in a blur. He sweeps her off her feet and up into the fold of his dress robes. I stand up to greet him with a handshake and a hug. My mother slides in behind us and kisses the man over her daughter's head. We share a family moment huddled in close. When we finally step back, I see a new expression on my father's face, one I have never seen before. Underneath his joyous, happy-to-be-home smile is a nervous energy akin to dread. He taught me to look for these things in others when in negotiation, but to see it on him is so foreign.

"It's good to be home," he says as he ruffles my sister's hair. He looks at me with a warm smile.

"How was the Solstice, my love?" my mother says as she takes his hand.

My father's eyes fall to the floor at her question. I feel a lump in my throat. *Something big is coming.* "Eventful," he finally says. He lets go of Analise and Mother and takes his seat on his throne. He then beckons for Mother to join him at his side; she does. My sister and I stand in front of them. My father rests his elbows on the armrests of the throne and grips his own hands tightly. When he raises his eyes up finally, he speaks again, "I have news."

"What is it, Father?" I say quietly.

The High Lord's lips purse. He seems so uneasy to speak. I have never seen anything like it. He looks old on the throne. My mother's face loses a bit of color as she pats his arm, motioning for him to tell us. After a long silence, he sighs. "At the Winter Solstice, we found a mortal girl within our midst masquerading as a traveling musician."

"I'm sorry, a mortal girl?" Mother interjects incredulously. "A mortal girl in the Upper Realm?"

"Are you serious, Father?" I ask over top of her. My mind is racing. *How could a mortal make it that far into the realm without being caught? I* start mentally analyzing who we need to speak to shore up our defenses at the border and how many Fae we need to send.

"Yes. She was apprehended and made to stand the Duel of the Heirs."

"She's been taken care of then?" I raise an eyebrow. To my surprise, my father looks away from me and around the room. He remains silent. I repeat my question. "She's been taken care of? Do we need to worry about retaliation from the… mortals?" I almost chuckle at the absurdity of the idea. "The threat has been neutralized, right?" I can't imagine a mortal girl taking down a multitude of Fae heirs even without all of them present.

"Not exactly," he answers tentatively. "The girl exhibited intense magical power and… leveled the field."

"She has magic?" My mother and I exclaim in unison. Analise's eyes go wide as her mouth falls open. "There's no way," I exclaim. "She would have to be a—"

"A half-Fae," the High Lord interrupts. "And she is. She is… my daughter."

There is a high-pitched, intense ringing in my ears. My vision grows small and narrow as I focus on my father's solemn face. I feel like the air is being sucked from my lungs. *Another child... Another daughter.*

Then I see my mother's face, and I am abruptly brought out of my stupor. She is horrified and crushed and furious all in one expression. "Your daughter?" she forces through her teeth.

"Elise, I—"

"Your daughter, Alexander?" Her voice raises. "She can't be your daughter because you have been with me since we were engaged. You never slept with another woman."

"Elise, please let me explain—"

"Why should I let you explain? Why should I let you continue to stand here and stumble over your words when you have dropped this tidbit of information as casually as if you were discussing afternoon tea?" My mother's eyes are furious now, her hands vibrating slightly. If she doesn't get control of her emotions, her magic could explode and turn this whole thing into a much bigger mess. I turn to Analise and kneel down to her level. "Hey sis, I think Mom and Dad need to—"

"No," my father says. "She needs to stay. She needs to hear all of this to understand." I slowly rise to my feet. He turns to my mother and looks her in the eye. She looks like she is staring right past him. "Before… we were married, I took a trip to the Middle Realm. I met a young woman, and she took me on a wild tour of the city. We… we were close. I was only there for a few weeks, but I began to fall for her. I tried to leave before it got to be too intense, but she convinced me to stay one more night. The mortal girl… Grace… she is our daughter."

My mother pushes to her feet, but my father blocks her from leaving the throne area. She fights against him, trying to flee. He holds fast. "Elise, I left her because I wanted to marry you. We have two beautiful children; I have loved my life with you." She stops her struggle, but when her face looks up, I can see fierce tears in her eyes. The anger bubbles up in my chest. I wish he would stop looking at her with so much love. He betrayed her; he doesn't get to… keep looking at her like that.

"Why…" she forces her voice through her teeth, "Why would you bring her here?"

The man gulps slowly. "She's… 19."

At that moment, my world falls away completely.

"I didn't know she was… the law states that…"

"No." I thought I was thinking the word, but apparently I said it out loud because everyone turns to look at me. "You're not giving her the heirship."

"Son, I am sorry, I don't have a—"

"Of course you have a choice!" I explode. "She knows nothing about this world; she wouldn't know how to lead."

"It is the law, Neil. Upper Realm law. We would lose legitimacy in the eyes of the other Houses. The House of the Evening would be ruined."

"We'll be ruined anyway!"

There is nothing else I can say or do but leave. My father is too far away to stop me. I run straight out of the throne room and up the front stairs. The hallways blur together as I make my way towards my room. This is just too much to process. *How is it possible? Why did it have to be before the wedding? Why does she have to be older? The girl can't just come in here and take everything I have worked for, everything I have been trained for. This isn't fair!* I keep running. Everything looks blurry in my detached mind.

But when I pass by the library, I see a flash of reddish-brown hair browsing the shelves and I stop short. *Is that her?* I back up slowly and move into the doorway. The girl doesn't look like much. She's not delicate enough looking to have any type of good breeding, but she's not sturdy like a warrior either. Her shoulders are tense as she looks out the big window over the valley. I'm seeing red. She doesn't deserve to be standing here in that room, in *my* home.

"So," the word slips out of my lips before I can say it harshly. "You're her?"

Grace whips around to look at me. I stare her down. "Excuse me?" she asks. I feel the anger mounting inside me when I see my father's eyes on her face.

"You're that *mortal* girl."

"Who the hell are you?" *Now I see it.*

I stand up tall, trying to be intimidating. "I'm Neil Sonra Faelie, the oldest of the *true* House of the Evening bloodline."

She sighs. "Ah. So you're the half-brother."

My body takes over, and I move quickly into the room. "You took away everything from me." She steps back, and I relish the fear in her eyes. "I'm the heir to the throne, not you. I've been training my entire life to take Dad's place, and you come in with your uncontrollable powers and your fucking half-mortal blood to take away what is rightfully mine." She looks taken aback, but the fury is building and all I want to do is wrap my hands around her throat.

"Look, Neil…"

I interrupt her. "No. You better watch your back, *sis*." I sneer. "I'm gunning for you." I reach out and shove her back slightly. To my satisfaction, she stumbles.

But then I see something in her eyes. A flash of fury, bigger than what I feel in my chest. She hauls off and shoves me hard with a growl in her throat. I hit the floor, barely catching myself from slamming my head into the ground. "Listen to me, you pompous piece of Fae shit," she hisses. "I didn't ask for this!" Before I can take a breath, she starts screaming at me. "I didn't ask for any of this! I was perfectly happy in my little mortal world with my mother and my brother! I never needed to know any of this!" All the while, she's backing me up to the doorway into the wall beside it. "But you, Fae scum like you, took my brother from me. And then you lied about what happened to him. You forced me to come to this world and find out for myself!"

She pokes me in the chest. Her finger jabs like a knife. "*Our father…*" There is so much venom in her voice. I can't help but be in awe of it. "Abandoned me as a child. I don't remember him at all. At least you got to grow up knowing who you were. I'm being thrown into this Lady-forsaken world with no direction, no instruction, and now I'm the heir to a fucking Fae House."

Grace leans in close to me. The heat of her breath is agitating, but I don't dare move. With uncontrollable magic, there's no telling what might make her snap. I'm trying to intimidate her, not get killed. "So I would be very careful about who you are threatening. My uncontrollable powers might just slip and take your Lady-damned head off." She pushes me one more time into the wall, and I get to my feet. "Save your petty threats for some other bitch. I have bigger things to deal with than a jealous child like you."

"Get out," she says. "Now." I try to speak again, but she shrieks *"Get out now! Leave me alone!"* I see her hands start to shake, so I run out of the room.

My ire has died down after the confrontation, but my heart is still pounding in my chest. I don't care that she's here. I don't care that she is now the heir. I will take back what is rightfully mine, one way or another. *She can't take this from me. No matter what she thinks she can do. I will petition my father; I'll petition every High Lord in the realm if I have to. I will take every avenue I can think of to get them to change that law.*

I will make Father see that his *real* child should be on the House of the Evening throne and not that bastard mortal. It's just a matter of time.

Acknowledgments

I would love to thank Angela R. Watts for doing a fantastic job on editing and proofreading this book and Milan Krstevski for a fantastic cover redesign. I also want to thank C.S. Ratliff, my original cover designer who put together a great first cover. I want to thank my beta readers for giving me such constructive feedback: my sister, Morgan; my friends, Diana and Cassie, and my author friend, Laura. E. Thompson. Finally, I would like to thank my family and my boyfriend, Daniel for their support during my entire publishing journey.

About the Author

Cady Hammer has been a writer for most of her life. From the time she was eleven years old writing her first novel between classes, she always looked to the world to bring inspiration. She was often teased for being in her own world, but never hesitated to invite others along on the adventure. She graduated from the College of William and Mary with a Bachelor of Arts in History and is now pursuing a Master of Arts in Public History.

Cady is the author of the Chasing Fae Trilogy and loves to create stories that take people away from the world for a while. She creates her universes with inspiration from her studies, trying to create a place that feels so real that readers have to explore it. These stories explore the complexities of relationships crafted around the idea that love, friendship, and grief are all interwoven. She hopes to one day become a bestselling author alongside her desired career in museum work.

You can connect with me on:

- https://cadyhammer.com
- https://twitter.com/CadyHammer
- https://facebook.com/cadyhammerauthor
- https://instagram.com/cadyhammerauthor
- https://pinterest.com/cadyahammer

Subscribe to my newsletter:

- https://fluffaboutfantasy.com/subscribe

Also by Cady Hammer

Check out these other works!

Chasing Fae

Grace Richardson is a young mortal woman whose only concerns are providing for her family, playing her violin, and spending as much time as possible with her brother, Leo. When Leo goes into service in the Fae's world as a mercenary, she expects him to return with the honor that he deserves.

When Leo suddenly dies in an unspecified accident, not a word, medal, or penny comes down from the higher-ups. Suspecting foul play, Grace disguises herself as a Fae and sneaks into the Upper Realm to get some answers. She anticipates being in way over her head, but the Fae soldier who discovers her true identity only a day in? Not so much.

Now Grace is forced to drag Aiden along as she tries to work out exactly how and why her brother died. Along the way, she has no choice but to confront her prejudices against the Fae as she attempts to sort out the difference between the honest and the dishonest. Political conspiracies, demon realm escapades, and family secrets will all lead Grace to the answers she's looking for… and some that she isn't.

Chasing War

Expect the unexpected when you take your place in Fae society.

When Grace arrives at the House of the Evening, she is instantly thrust into the world of the Fae nobility. As the heir to a throne she didn't even realize was hers, she has to navigate magical education, complex traditions, and a stepfamily she never asked for. With her new tutor, Talon, and Aiden by her side, Grace steps out into the Upper Realm as Lady of the House of the Evening only to find a war exploding under her gaze led by the House of Darkness. With minimal training and outdated laws keeping her from stepping up for the war effort, she and Aiden must quickly strategize against the invaders while searching in earnest for the remaining six prophecy members. As the war rages on and more pieces of the puzzle fall into place, Grace must make a decision about who to trust and how to lead.

Chasing Fate

"We are on our own now ... From here on out, we win or lose on our own merit. We either save the realm, or we condemn it to burn."

With the war in the Upper Realm in full swing, Grace has her hands full fighting for a society that has only just begun to accept her as its own. The House of Darkness and High Lord Carron only grow stronger, and with demonic magic involved, there's no telling what havoc the enemy plans to wreak across the Three Realms. She has no time to think about Aiden's return to the House of the Evening and her conflicting feelings for him. And there's no time to confront Faolan about the kiss they shared and what might be brewing between them. There are battles to fight, lands to liberate, and, most importantly, an all-too-pressing prophecy to decipher.

Caught in a vicious cycle of victory and defeat, Grace has to confront her heritage once and for all and fulfill the prophecy with her friends by any means necessary, whether or not it is the fate that she desires for herself.

The Ivy Labyrinth: Volume 1

Kristy Fitzpatrick just can't catch a break.

As a mortal in a magical world, she often feels disconnected from the rest of her mystical, more exciting classmates. The only thing that she has to compete with in the classroom is her mind.

But even for a magical being like her impulsive naiad best friend, Brianna, life is far from stable. Centuries ago, when a fully formed labyrinth sprang from the ocean, the magic emanating from its ivy walls caused all kinds of devastating magical consequences that affect the planet every year from magical instability in beings all over the world to chaotic natural disasters.

Every year, four high school students are chosen to enter the labyrinth and try to break its hold on the world by solving a series of complex riddles and challenges. Most never come out.

But when Kristy's school is selected as the home of the next four students, despite her lack of choice in the matter, she sees an opportunity to do something that no other student has managed to do so far: survive the labyrinth.

In Volume 1 of this Hunger Games-meets-Maze Runner high fantasy story from Kindle Vella and Radish, Kristy is about to learn whether her mind and body are up to the task. Because somehow, as she tests her own limitations, the Labyrinth is learning how to best her and her companions. There is no telling what kind of obstacles could come next.

The Ivy Labyrinth: Volume 2

Brianna is fed up.

It isn't enough for this Ivy Labyrinth and its never-ending stream of challenges to have ripped her away from her loving family and bright future. It just will not stop throwing her into situations with popular asshole, Ash. He keeps making nice with her best friend, Kristy, and discussing academic and logic puzzles like he hasn't spent the last three years goofing off in all of his classes. On top of that, when Kai and Kristy are forced to stay behind after a Sphinx's riddle goes awry, he has the gall to trust her and follow her judgment completely during a dangerous situation. But whenever she tries to have a basic conversation, he blows her off and avoids her like the plague. Well, as much as one can be avoided while being forced together in a maze. As she tries to peel away Ash's layers to find the truth underneath, Brianna finds herself facing her own secrets that she has tried so hard to bury. For the first time, she will have to confront whether or not she could have been very, very wrong about the boy she has despised for their entire educational lives.

The Ivy Labyrinth

Cady Hammer

The Ivy Labyrinth

Updates regularly on Kindle Vella and Radish.

In a world of magical instability, four high school students are chosen every year to enter the Ivy Labyrinth and try to break its hold on the planet by solving a series of complex challenges and riddles. Most never come out. Now, a new four have been chosen: the quiet intellectual, Kristy; the dutiful son, Kai; the impulsive best friend, Brianna; and the highly reactive screwup, Ash. In a high fantasy, Hunger Games-meets-Maze Runner serial, there's no telling what obstacles will come up next.